SONA SHARMA

LOOKING AFTER
PLANET EARTH

Other books by Chitra Soundar

A Dollop of Ghee and a Pot of Wisdom
A Jar of Pickles and a Pinch of Justice
A Sliver of Moon and a Shard of Truth
Sona Sharma, Very Best Big Sister

Contents

START SMALL, START NOW

Sona Sharma lives in a large joint family full of happy people who argue sometimes. Relatives come unannounced, the phone rings often and everyone is always welcome whatever time it is.

These are Sona's people:

Amma – Sona's mum. She is a music teacher and singer. She's always humming a song or listening to music.

Appa – Sona's dad. He works with computers all day and sometimes at night too.

Thatha – Sona's grandfather. He knows a lot of things. And when he doesn't know about something he tells a story about something else.

Paatti – Sona's grandmother. She makes the best sweets in the whole world. She always laughs at Thatha's jokes.

The President – Sona's other grandmother. Sona doesn't know her real name. The President used to be the president of some college, so everyone calls her that still. She lives in the only orange house in the entire neighbourhood, called The Orange.

Joy and Renu – Sona's friends from school. They live a street away and go to school with Sona in an auto-rickshaw.

Mullai – Sona's auto-rickshaw driver. She picks up Sona, Joy and Renu in that order, to drop off at school. In the evening she takes them home – Renu first, Joy next and Sona last. She's never late and recites a lot of Tamil poetry.

Elephant – Sona's best friend. He fits perfectly in Sona's toy bag and her cuddly chair and next to her on her pillow. Sona never goes anywhere without him, except, of course, to school.

◈

It was Friday morning and Sona was in class. She was sitting in the front with Joy and Renu.

"Good morning, everyone," said their teacher, Miss Rao. "Today we're going to talk about Planet Earth."

Sona loved Planet Earth so she listened carefully. She didn't want to miss a thing.

"Our Planet Earth is in trouble," said Miss Rao. "Our summers are getting hotter and our rainy seasons are causing more floods. Scientists have been studying this and they believe our planet is heating up—"

"Heating up?" interrupted Joy.

"Yes," said Miss Rao. "More cars on the road cause more heat in the air."

"And more smoke," said Renu.

"That's right," said Miss Rao. "And our oceans are polluted too."

"I love going to the beach," said Sona. "But the waves bring a lot of rubbish back."

"Yes, that's because we throw a lot of our rubbish into the ocean," said Miss Rao.

"I don't," said Sona. "Paatti always makes me bring the rubbish back in a bag."

"That's good, Sona," said Miss Rao.

In Geography, Miss Rao showed them photos of melting polar ice and talked about why that was a bad thing. In Science, they learned that some rubbish lived for ever.

"Like what, Miss?" asked Sona.

"Plastic bottles," said Miss Rao. "And babies' nappies."

Sona worried about Minmini's nappies living for ever and ever and stinking for ever and ever.

In Maths, they did sums about forests disappearing.

I don't think Elephant will like these sums very much, thought Sona.

P e ople pollute
O Cean And
L a ND,
L ooTiNG
U nnecEssaRily
T AkiNG
I mpoLiTeLy
O veR and OveR From
N ATurE

In English, they wrote poems about pollution.

"Our planet is in trouble," said Renu.

"But we can fix it," said Miss Rao. "If everyone helps."

"Even children?" asked Sona.

"Yes, especially children," said Miss Rao. "Start small, start now."

Sona didn't understand. She raised her hand and asked Miss Rao to explain.

"When we leave our class and go to play," Miss Rao said, "what do we do?"

"Bump into each other," said Renu.

"Before that," said Miss Rao, chuckling.

"We switch off the lights and fans," said Sona, pointing at the sign near the door.

"Exactly," said Miss Rao. "Where do we throw our unwanted paper and cardboard?"

"In the recycling bin," said Joy.

Miss Rao nodded. "Yes, we have to do that at home too," she said. "If we all look after our planet, we can make a difference. Let's make a pledge. Repeat after me: 'I – insert your name' – and then say what you will do…"

"I, Sona Sharma, will look after Planet Earth," said Sona.

And then Joy pledged, and then Renu and the rest of the class.

"So, what could we do about it when we get home?" asked Miss Rao. "Any ideas?"

"I'll ask my entire family to look after Planet Earth," said Sona.

"Good idea, Sona," said Miss Rao. "Maybe all of us can work out a plan for our families. Those who bring them in on Monday will receive a gold star."

That evening, when they were returning home in the auto-rickshaw with Mullai,

Joy said, "I love getting gold stars."

"Me too," said Renu.

"Me too," said Sona. "But even if Miss wasn't giving out gold stars, I'd still want to look after our planet."

Joy and Renu agreed.

The moment Paatti opened the door, Sona declared, "I'm going to look after Planet Earth and I'm going to ask everyone to help."

"Excellent," said Paatti. "I'm sure we can all help you."

Sona woke up on Saturday morning to a very quiet house.

"Where is everyone?" she asked.

"Maybe they have gone away on holiday," said Elephant.

Sona tiptoed over to see Minmini, who was sleeping in her cradle. Surely her family wouldn't leave Sona, Minmini and Elephant and go on holiday.

Besides, it was December and the season of music. Amma sang at concerts. Paatti and the President took turns to look after Minmini. Sona helped too. She came up with silly songs that made Minmini smile and giggle.

Sona went downstairs. Paatti was in the garden.

"What is Paatti doing?" asked Elephant.

"She is creating a kolam. She uses rice flour to draw designs of all sorts of things, like flowers, pots and mangoes."

"Why can't she draw on paper?" asked Elephant. Elephants didn't know about kolams.

"Kolams are drawn on the ground inside or outside our home," said Sona.

Every morning Sona woke up to the sound of Paatti's broom sweeping the street outside their gate. Then Paatti washed the area with water and drew a kolam. Some days she created large designs and some days she drew small ones. During festivals, she made special kolams for the particular celebration.

Sona watched Paatti mark out a square of dots. Then she drew squiggles around the dots to make a squiggly pattern.

"If I had to walk along the lines of a kolam, 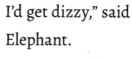 I'd get dizzy," said Elephant.

"Never walk on a kolam – you'd smudge it," said Sona.

Paatti stood up. "What do you think?" she asked.

"It's beautiful!" said Sona. "But why are you drawing it here and not in front of the house?"

"Because I'm practising for the annual kolam competition," said Paatti. "Don't you remember? I drew a lamp kolam for last year's competition."

Sona nodded. "Sort of," she said.

Paatti had filled the ground with kolam designs. Her white dots and squiggles made beautiful patterns on the brown soil.

"Don't step on them," said Paatti. "I'll pick one of these to draw on the morning of the competition."

Thatha came into the garden. "I see you're getting ready for the competition," he said. "Sona, did I tell you I'm the chief judge this year?"

"So, will you give first prize to Paatti?" asked Sona.

"Not necessarily," said Thatha. "Judges have to be impartial to be fair."

Thatha was also part of the dawn choir group called the Pasuram Party. The group sang songs written by Saint Andal, a poet who had lived hundreds of years ago. Some of the members started out at five in the morning.

They gathered the others as they walked from house to house until they reached the local temple. Paatti explained that the dawn choir was the judging panel for the kolam competition.

"It's a neighbourhood competition," said Paatti, "so everyone knows someone on the judging panel."

"And it's for fun," said Thatha.

"But I take it very seriously," said Paatti.

Thatha chuckled. "Sona and you are exactly the same. You take everything seriously!"

"That's not a bad thing!" protested Paatti.

"Paatti," said Sona, "will you show me how to draw a kolam?"

"Of course," said Paatti. She pinched a bit of rice flour between her finger and thumb and drew on the ground.

Then Sona had a go. She loved drawing with pencils, pens and paintbrushes. But drawing with rice flour was not as easy.

"Practice makes perfect," said Paatti. "Keep trying."

Elephant watched as Sona got better and better. "Practice makes perfect," he whispered.

Every Little Helps

After lunch, Sona remembered that she had to make a gold star plan for school, to look after the planet. She took out a notepad and pencil and picked up Elephant. She was determined to make the best plan she could.

First, she went to her grandparents' room. Thatha and Paatti were napping. Sona switched off the whirring ceiling fan that kept them cool.

Then she inspected Thatha's shelves and wrote something down in her notebook.

After that, she went to her parents' room. Amma wasn't there but Minmini was in her cradle.

Sona said to Minmini, "Did you know your nappies never, ever get destroyed?"

Minmini said, "Mmm."

"Do you want to do something about it?" asked Sona.

"Mmm," Minmini said again.

"I'll help you," said Sona, picking up a bag.

"What are you doing?" asked Elephant.

"Minmini needs that."

"Shh!" said Sona.

"Minmini is my sister and she wants to look after our planet too."

"She can't even look after herself yet," said Elephant.

But Sona wasn't listening. She was already on her way to Appa's study, where Appa was playing a video game. Sona tiptoed to the switchboard without Appa noticing and turned off his game.

"Run!" she shouted to Elephant.

"You're carrying me," said Elephant. "You run – fast!"

They went to the kitchen. Sona checked the shelves. The pots, the spice containers and even the drinking tumblers were made of stainless steel. That's when she saw the dustpan. A plastic dustpan.

Before she could check anything else, she heard noises. Loud noises. Thatha-and-Appa-being-very-upset kind of noises. Sona darted through the back door into the garden and sat down on the bench. She opened a new page in her notebook and began to doodle.

Appa and Thatha were being very loud.

"It's very hot in here!" said Thatha. "Is there a power cut?"

"Looks like it," said Appa. "My video game got switched off."

"That's strange," said Thatha.

Appa checked the switchboard and the switch for the fan.

"Someone has turned these off," said Appa.

Paatti laughed. "Sona must be looking after Planet Earth," she said.

"Uh-oh!" said Elephant. "You're going to be in trouble."

"Shh!" said Sona.

Then everything went quiet except the whirr of the ceiling fan.

"They just turned everything back on," said Elephant. "And now they're wasting electricity again. Don't they care about the planet?"

"We will make them care," said Sona. "I promise."

Sona drew Elephant climbing a tree (even

though elephants don't do that), Elephant riding a bicycle (elephants must not be made to do that) and Elephant snoozing (which is Elephant's favourite thing to do).

"I think it's safe to go back inside now," said Elephant.

Sona tiptoed into the kitchen to fetch a drink.

"Nidhi!" shouted Appa, calling for Amma. "I can't find the nappies and Minmini has a stinky bottom."

Sona was so startled she almost dropped her tumbler of water. She peeped into the living room.

Amma was there, preparing for a concert. She looked up from her songbook and shouted back, "They're where they always are!"

Elephant nudged Sona. "Are they?"

"Shh!" said Sona.

"Unless we've switched to invisible nappies, they're definitely not here," said Appa. "I might faint of poo smell."

Sona giggled.

"Do you want Appa to faint of poo smell?" asked Elephant.

"Shh!" said Sona.

Amma grumbled as she went upstairs. Sona and Elephant followed.

"That's strange," said Amma. "They were just here."

Sona scuttled into her room, sat on the bed and picked up a book. A book worked without electricity and was not harmful to the planet.

The door handle rattled. Elephant hid under a pillow.

Appa barged in. Amma, Paatti and Thatha barged in behind him.

"You didn't knock, Appa," said Sona.

"You didn't ask for permission before you switched off my game," said Appa.

"And you didn't ask before you switched off

the fan – and my amazing dream," said Thatha.
"You must practise what you preach, Sona!"

Sona shrugged.

"And what about the
nappies?" asked Paatti.

"I thought you were
potty-trained, Sona,"
joked Appa.

"Appa! I didn't take
them to use them," said
Sona. "Did you know
that nappies live in the
rubbish for ever?"

"Huh?" grunted Appa.

"When you throw a baby's nappy into the bin,
it goes into landfill, Appa," said Sona.

*If humans had to fill land with anything, why not
with trees?* thought Elephant.

"So, I explained it to Minmini and she agreed
to give up her nappies."

Appa sighed. "Where are the nappies, Sona?"
he asked.

"Under my bed," said Sona. "But I'm not returning them."

"Family meeting in the living room in ten minutes," said Appa. "As soon as I change Minmini."

"But—"

"Now hand me the bag of nappies," said Appa.

Appa had his I'm-the-grown-up-and-I-make-the-rules voice.

Reluctantly, Sona handed him the bag. Sometimes grown ups got their own way even if they were wrong.

"Appa is so upset," said Elephant. "Will he make you stop looking after the planet?"

"I'm never going to stop," said Sona. "I'm going to make a plan and show it to everyone in the family meeting."

Ten minutes later, everyone gathered in the living room for the family meeting. Even Minmini.

Thatha called it the Panchayat – the meeting of five leaders – just like the ones in his native village.

Appa cleared his throat. "I've brought a complaint to this meeting," he said.

"Is the complaint about me?" asked Sona.

"About your actions," said Appa. "We never blame the person. We only want them to correct their actions."

"You may state your complaint," said Thatha.

"My complaint is that Sona switched off your fan, pulled the plug on my game and hid Minmini's nappies without permission."

"I want to look after Planet Earth," said Sona.

31

"Miss Rao asked us to make a plan for our entire family to follow. If we all do a little bit, we can make a difference."

Thatha wiped his glasses with his handkerchief. "Sona is right," he said. "Remember how the squirrel got his three stripes?"

Thatha was going to tell a story. And Sona had a feeling it would help everyone NOT be upset with her.

Thatha began. "When Prince Rama had to build a bridge to cross the ocean, he needed all the help he could get. He asked for the army of monkeys to help carry the rocks. A little squirrel wanted to help too, but he wasn't strong enough to carry the big rocks. So the squirrel carried pebbles to fill the gaps between the rocks. When the bridge was finished, the prince thanked everyone, including the squirrel. Rama gently stroked the squirrel's back with three fingers as he thanked him. Those three fingers made permanent stripes on the squirrel's back, reminding us that we all must help each other in every small way we can."

"See! That's what Miss Rao said," said Sona. "Start small, start now."

"OK, Sona, tell us your ideas," said Appa. "We'll help in any way we can."

"Yes, it's never too late to start doing good," said Thatha.

"I made a list," said Sona, spreading a sheet of paper on the table. "I have written down a task for each of you," she said. "Even Minmini."

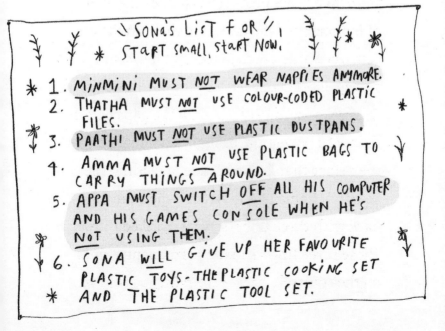

SONA'S LIST FOR
START SMALL, START NOW.

1. MINMINI MUST NOT WEAR NAPPIES ANYMORE.
2. THATHA MUST NOT USE COLOUR-CODED PLASTIC FILES.
3. PAATHI MUST NOT USE PLASTIC DUSTPANS.
4. AMMA MUST NOT USE PLASTIC BAGS TO CARRY THINGS AROUND.
5. APPA MUST SWITCH OFF ALL HIS COMPUTER AND HIS GAMES CONSOLE WHEN HE'S NOT USING THEM.
6. SONA WILL GIVE UP HER FAVOURITE PLASTIC TOYS - THE PLASTIC COOKING SET AND THE PLASTIC TOOL SET.

No one spoke for a few minutes.

"Maybe they don't like your ideas," whispered Elephant.

Sona wasn't sure what to do next. She was about to pull the paper off the table when Amma cleared her throat.

"If Minmini doesn't wear a nappy," said Amma, "she'd make her cradle dirty."

"And what about the smell?" said Appa. "Maybe we can move the cradle to Sona's room?"

Elephant nudged Sona. "I don't want poo in our room," he said.

Sona tapped the table with her pencil.

She remembered the old clothes Paatti had shown her when Minmini was born.

"Paatti, did you use nappies for Appa too?" she asked.

"In those days, we didn't have nappies," said Paatti. "We used soft cotton cloth."

Amma smiled. "That's a brilliant idea," she said. "We could do that too. We can wash them and use them over and over again. It's time to say goodbye to disposable nappies."

"We'll save money too," said Thatha. "What's your next idea, Sona?"

"Miss Rao said the plastic in the rubbish will live for ever," said Sona. "Your plastic files must go, Thatha."

"If we throw the plastic ones away, they'll just end up as landfill," said Appa. "But all new files can be cardboard ones."

Appa's solution was a good one.

Paatti agreed the plastic dustpans were not a good idea. "I'll get the bamboo dustpans in future, just like my mother used to have."

Amma agreed to switch to a cloth bag to carry her things.

"Can we recycle my favourite plastic cooking set and tool set too?" said Sona. "And, Amma, I don't want to get any more plastic toys, please."

Elephant thought Sona sounded a little sad.

Appa put an arm around her. "How about I share some of my real tools with you and show you how to use them safely?"

"Then I'll help you when you do repairs," said Sona, raising her hand to high-five Appa.

"And I'll find my play cooking set made of brass," said Amma. "It's in a crate somewhere in the loft."

"That'll be fun," said Sona. "I'll share that with Minmini too."

Paatti looked over the list and nodded. "We'll save on electricity if everyone switches off their devices when not in use," she said. "So definitely yes to that."

"But, Sona, don't switch off the fridge!" said Appa. "Not unless you want to have sour milk with your cereal."

Sona was so happy that everyone was coming up with such amazing ideas. "Thanks, everyone," said Sona. "For helping me – and the planet – with this plan."

"Mmm," said Minmini.

Easy-Peasy
Jalebi Squeezy

On Monday, Sona showed her PLANET EARTH
CARE PLAN to Renu and Joy. Renu and Joy had
made their own family plans too.

"You all get gold stars," said Miss Rao.

"Thank you, Miss," said Sona.

"If just three families can make so many
changes," said Miss Rao, "imagine the difference
our entire neighbourhood could make. Could we
knock on our neighbours' doors and ask them to
make a plan?"

"That's, like, millions of houses!" said Joy.

"What if some of the houses have monsters, or ghosts?" asked Renu. "Whoooo!"

"If only our neighbourhood had an assembly like we have at school," said Sona, "we could tell everyone about looking after Planet Earth."

They were still whispering about their gold star plans when they got into Mullai's auto-rickshaw after school.

"What's the big secret?" asked Mullai as she turned onto a quieter street.

"We're talking about looking after our planet," said Sona. "Do you have any ideas for us?"

"I'll have a think," replied Mullai. "In the meantime, you can help me think of a way I can avoid the kolams on the streets, especially the ones with coloured powders and glitter that sting my eyes. Such a nuisance!"

"You could get a flying auto-rickshaw," said Renu.

When Sona reached home, she wanted to gather more ideas for her plan. But her family was busy.

Amma was busy getting ready for her concert. Paatti was busy watching videos about new kolam designs. Thatha was busy getting ready to go to a judges' meeting.

"I'm not busy," said Elephant.

"Thanks!" said Sona. "Do you have any ideas about how to make everyone stop and think about looking after the planet?"

"Maybe you should stop and think about what they are doing," said Elephant. "Didn't Thatha say to practise what you preach?"

Elephant was right. If Sona helped Amma get ready for the concert and helped Paatti with the competition and helped Thatha with the judging, then maybe they'd stop and help Sona too.

Half an hour later, the doorbell rang. It was the President. She had come to pick Amma up for the concert. "I want to come too," said Sona.

"Sure," said Amma. "You can keep Minmini company."

"Can we walk to the concert?" asked Sona. The concert was taking place in the auditorium at Sona's school.

"Not today, Sona," said the President. "Your amma and I are wearing silk saris. And we have to bring Minmini too. The roads are too uneven for a pushchair. The streets are filled with kolams. It's best if we drive."

"But it's not good for the planet," said Sona.

The President didn't even respond. Elephant reminded Sona that she was practising what she was preaching. So, Sona grabbed Elephant and got into the car without any arguments.

The President turned to Sona and asked, "Is Paatti ready for the kolam competition?"

"She is preparing for it," said Sona.

"Last-minute preparations are not good," said the President with a snort. "I'm always prepared. I've already worked it all out and ordered everything I need."

"Sona, did you know the President has won three years in a row?" asked Amma.

"Wow!" said Sona. She had never won anything three years in a row ever.

Sona's school looked different in the evening. The corridors were silent and the classrooms were shut. Only the auditorium was busy and bustling with people. Amma, the President, Sona and Minmini followed the signs to the green room.

The green room wasn't actually green. It was just a small room where performers waited until it was time to go onstage.

"You can wait here with me too," said Amma. "The President usually stays here with Minmini until I'm ready to go on."

Amma wore headphones and sat with her eyes closed. The President was reading a book.

Minmini was asleep in her car-seat cradle. Sona was bored. Elephant was bored too.

"Come, I'll show you round my school," said Sona to Elephant, getting up to leave.

"Sona, don't leave the hall," said the President. "I want to be able to peep out and spot you."

"OK," said Sona.

Elephant was excited. This was where Sona came when she left him at home every day.

The hall was brightly lit. The sound system was blaring out the beats of a mridangam. Appa used to play the mridangam before he started playing video games.

Sona saw Miss Rao, who was waving. "Hello, Miss Rao," said Sona.

"Hello, Sona," said Miss Rao. "I wondered if I'd see you here this evening. I'm in charge of the sound system. Would you like to help?"

"Yes, please," said Sona.

"Yes, please," whispered Elephant.

Sona followed Miss Rao to the back of the auditorium.

"Sona, do you remember these from when we did our class play?" asked Miss Rao. "The red button will turn off all the microphones, this one'll turn off the speakers and this dial will increase or decrease the volume. These switches you flip to turn on and off each of the microphones on stage."

"Yes, I remember," said Sona.

Soon, a lady wearing a purple sari came onstage.

"That's Mrs Pillai," said Miss Rao. "She's the organizer of this concert."

Miss Rao switched off the mridangam music and turned on the stage mics.

Mrs Pillai welcomed the audience for the evening's concert. Then she talked about how wonderful Nidhi Sharma's singing was.

"That's my amma she's talking about," said Sona.

"I know," said Miss Rao.

"I know," whispered Elephant.

Then Mrs Pillai reminded everyone to switch off their mobile phones. At that very instant, a phone rang.

"Please switch off the phone!" Mrs Pillai shouted.

Everyone looked around to see whose phone it was.

"I think it's Miss Rao's phone," whispered Elephant.

Sona listened. Yes, Elephant was right.

"Miss," said Sona, "I think it's your phone."

"Oops!" said Miss Rao. She pulled it out and checked the display. "I've got to take this."

The phone was still ringing.

"Switch it off or please take your call outside," shrieked Mrs Pillai.

Miss Rao sighed. "Please can you switch off

Mrs Pillai's mic when she finishes talking by flipping this switch, then turn on this mic for your amma?"

Sona nodded.

"Good girl. Thank you," said Miss Rao, hurrying out to the corridor to take her call.

"Turn this off, turn that on," said Sona. "Easy-peasy jalebi squeezy!"

SUPER PROUD

Mrs Pillai forgot about the concert in her outburst about the "menace of mobile phones". Sona waited for her to finish. Elephant waited. The audience waited. She didn't stop.

Mrs Pillai ranted louder and louder about how everyone was "always on their mobile phones in buses and auto-rickshaws and even in the cinema". Sona grew restless. Elephant grew restless. The audience grew restless.

"When will Amma sing?" asked Elephant.

Sona didn't know.

SCREEECH!

Mrs Pillai had gotten too close to the microphone, shouting, "Mobile phones should be banned!"

"Can you make her less loud?" asked Elephant.

"Let me try," said Sona. She turned the volume dial to the left.

SCREEECH!

"Sorry!" cried Sona. She turned it the other way. The hall fell quiet.

"That's better," said Elephant.

"We can't hear Mrs Pillai," someone said.

"That's an added bonus," said someone else. "We can save our eardrums and electricity."

Yes! No mic means saving electricity, thought Sona. Maybe no lights would mean saving even more electricity?

Sona stood up on the chair and reached for the lights.

"Miss Rao didn't give you permission to turn off the lights," said Elephant.

"She was the one who told me to look after Planet Earth," said Sona.

"She definitely did," said Elephant.

"Do you know which switch it is?" asked Elephant.

"Whichever one I can reach," whispered Sona. She flipped the biggest switch on the panel.

Uh-oh!

The entire hall went dark.

At first the hall went quiet.

Then someone said, "Power cut!"

Another shouted, "Call Miss Rao! She must check the fuse."

The hall was full of angry shadows. Sona sat with Elephant behind the sound desk happy that they were saving electricity.

It was then that Miss Rao sprinted into the hall like an Olympic athlete. She checked the controls and turned on the lights and the mic. Everyone sat back in their seats and started chatting among themselves.

Miss Rao turned to Sona, who was sitting quietly and said, "You! Come with me."

"Uh-oh! We're in big trouble," said Elephant.

Miss Rao led Sona and Elephant to the green room. She told Amma and the President what had just happened.

"Didn't Appa tell you, you needed to ask before doing these things without permission?" asked Amma.

"Sorry," said Sona.

The President cleared her throat. "Sona, you've caused chaos during your amma's concert!" she said. "I want you to apologize to the audience."

Sona's eyes filled with tears.

"There's no need for that," said Miss Rao. "I'll tell everyone there was a problem with the system."

"No," said the President. "Sona, let this be a lesson. Go and tell everyone that you're sorry."

Elephant thought the President was being super rude. Sona tried to stop the tears but they fell down her cheeks as if she had turned on a tap.

Amma hugged Sona. "You don't have to do that," she said.

The President grunted. "Nidhi, you spoil her too much," she muttered.

"Mum! Don't be like that," said Amma, taking Sona's side. "It's one thing to tell her off in private. It's another thing to do it in public."

"You're too soft," said the President. "Sona, you have to learn to take responsibility for your actions."

"Mum!" said Amma sternly. "Drop it."

Sona didn't want Amma and the President to fight. And the President was right. If Sona had made a mistake, she must own up to it.

"I'll do it," she said.

"You don't have to," said Amma.

"I want to," replied Sona.

Amma kissed Sona on the forehead.

She knew how hard it would be for Sona to go up onto the stage and apologize.

Sona and Elephant opened the door and went towards the front of the hall.

"You're so brave," whispered Elephant.

"No, I'm not," said Sona. "My legs are shaking like the time I gave the class speech at assembly."

"Then why are you doing it?" asked Elephant.

"Because I don't want the President to be upset with Amma," said Sona. "And I can explain to everyone why I did it."

"I'll come with you," said Miss Rao, catching up with Sona and Elephant.

Onstage, Sona stood on tiptoes to speak into the microphone. She leaned in and knocked on the mic.

SCREECH!

The hall quietened.

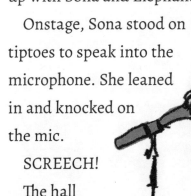

"I'm sorry I turned off the mic and lights," she said.

"Good girl," said Miss Rao, trying to nudge her away from the mic.

But Sona wouldn't budge. She had to tell everyone it wasn't a prank. She was just trying to look after the planet.

"My friends and I are very worried about Planet Earth," she said into the mic. "What if the planet gets too hot by the time we grow up? What if the oceans are so dirty that we can never go to the beach? We must all do something to protect our planet – switch off lights and speakers, find alternatives to plastic. It just piles up in landfill and never dies."

Sona couldn't go on. She wiped her nose and face on her sleeve and tried not to cry. Her legs were still trembling.

Miss Rao came to her rescue. "Sona's class has been working on a project about looking after the planet," she said. "They've been discovering that we can all help. Every little action goes a long way – like turning off lights when we don't need them or walking to the auditorium instead of driving if we live close by. Start small, start now," said Miss Rao.

"Do more, do it now," said Sona into the mic. Then she ran off the stage to the green room.

But inside the green room, the President sat like a simmering pot of sambhar full of chillies. "What a drama, Sona! You should be ashamed of yourself," she said.

"Sona is looking after our planet. And she has bravely apologized to an entire hall full of strangers. There is nothing to be ashamed of."

Sona smiled. Amma was on her side.

Then Amma got up to go to the stage. While Amma sang, Sona, Minmini and the President watched from the wings.

"That's our amma," whispered Sona to Minmini.

"Mmm," said Minmini.

Later that evening, when Amma pulled up at The Orange, the President turned to Sona. "A rule is a rule, Sona. We must all follow the rules established by our elders," she said. "We can't change them every which way we want."

Then she got out of the car, turned on her heels and went inside, without saying goodbye or goodnight. That made Sona cry again.

Amma hugged Sona and wiped her tears.

"I'm sorry, Amma," said Sona. "I just want to protect the planet."

"I know, darling," said Amma. "The President will come around. She loves the planet too."

Sona couldn't stop crying. Elephant wanted to make her feel better. But he didn't know how.

"It was brave of you to apologize in front of everyone," said Amma. "But it was even braver to ask everyone to join you in making changes. We need more children like you to show adults when we are wrong."

"So, you're not mad?" asked Sona, sniffling a little.

"Of course not," said Amma. "I'm proud of you. Super proud."

"I'm proud of you too," said Elephant. "Super proud."

Sona hugged Amma.

Elephant hugged Sona too.

<hr/>

The next day after school, Sona and Elephant sat in the garden watching squirrels race by. Minmini was also there, in her playpen.

"I can see the three stripes on the squirrels' backs," said Elephant, remembering the story Thatha had told them.

Sona didn't reply. Even though Amma wasn't mad at her, even though Miss Rao hadn't brought up the incident that day, Sona felt as if she had messed up.

"Hey, Sona!" Paatti called. "Would you like to help me with the competition?" Paatti showed Sona a notebook full of kolams she had been practising. "Every team is allowed one assistant. Your appa is always busy. Amma will have Minmini to look after. Thatha is the judge."

Sona smiled. "Will I be your assistant?" she asked. "We could be the Golden Team."

"Golden?" asked Paatti.

"Sona means gold. Your name, Kanaka, means gold too."

"Ah! Clever girl," said Paatti.

"Golden Team wins gold in kolam competition," said Sona in her best announcer voice.

"Mmm," said Minmini.

"Never look for a rainbow before the rain-clouds gather," said Paatti. "Don't celebrate too soon. The President uses coloured powders – Sesame Star, Mango Madness, Pumpkin Plume, Walnut Wish, Ginger Breeze."

"What about us?" asked Sona.

"We don't buy chemical colours," said Paatti.

Sona remembered something. "Mullai said the coloured powders irritate her eyes when she is driving," said Sona.

"Traditional kolams wouldn't do that," said Paatti. "I learned to draw traditional kolams from my grandmother and she learned from hers."

Sona flipped through Paatti's notebook of kolam designs. Each one consisted of squiggly lines weaving through a pattern of dots.

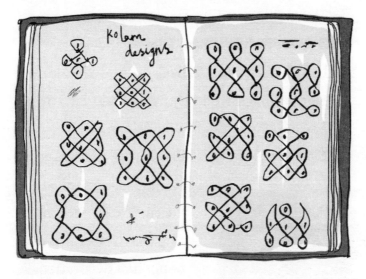

"Are all your kolams made of white squiggles and white dots?" asked Sona.

"Kolams can be any shape or drawing or picture," said Paatti. "But all my kolams are drawn with rice flour, just like my grandmother taught me."

Sona ran to the front gate and opened it.

She looked at the kolam Paatti had drawn that morning. It was a blazing sun. And Patti had placed a real yellow flower in the middle of the kolam sun.

"What's that?" asked Sona.

"That's the pumpkin flower stuck in a pot made of cow dung," said Paatti.

"Ugh!" said Sona. "Why?"

"So the flower won't fly away," said Paatti.

"But why cow dung?" asked Sona.

"Everything on that kolam is food for insects, bees and birds," said Paatti.

"The rice flour, the cow dung, the flower – they are not just decorations. They have a purpose. To feed the world around us."

"Paatti!" said Sona. "You're helping the planet with your kolams!"

Sona was even more excited to help Paatti now because Patti's kolam helped the creatures in their garden too.

᠃

The next day, when Sona was in the auto-rickshaw with Mullai on her way back from school, Sona was eager to tell Mullai about the rice flour kolams.

"I know," said Mullai. "Your amma and I used to draw with your paatti all the time. But we never won the competition. The people who used the chemical colours and glitter always won. So, I eventually lost interest."

That evening, Sona sat next to Baby Minmini while she lay in the cradle.

"Are we babysitting?" asked Elephant.

"No, we are just sitting with the baby," said Sona.

"Because Minmini is a very good listener."

Sona told Minmini about how Paatti didn't want to use harmful things in her kolam.

"If you ask me, people shouldn't be allowed to use anything harmful in the competition," said Elephant. "Only natural materials, like coconuts."

"We can't draw kolams with coconuts," said Sona. "But maybe we can do something about the chemicals and glitter."

"How?" asked Elephant.

"Jjjj," gurgled Minmini.

"Judge!" said Sona. "My grandfather is the chief judge. I'll ask him."

THE STATE OF KOLAM

Sona ran as fast as she could, down the stairs, through the living room, into the garden.

"Judge Thatha! Judge Thatha!" she shouted. "I have something important to tell you."

"What's exciting in Sona's world?"

"Ban chemicals," she said, gasping a little. "And the glitter and the plastic decorations."

"Slow down, take a breath and start from the beginning," said Thatha.

"You're the Judge of Kolams," said Sona.

"Old news," said Thatha.

Sona sat next to Thatha on the bench. "If we draw kolams with chemicals, use plastic decorations and glitter," she said, "where will it all go?"

"You tell me," said Thatha.

"The chemicals will fly up in the air that we breathe. The plastic and glitter will get washed down the drains into the oceans and kill the fish..."

Thatha listened. He was a good listener, like Minmini. He not only listened with his ears, he also listened with his eyes and his heart.

"And I guess you want me to fix this?" asked Thatha.

"You must ban them from the kolam competition," said Sona.

"I see," said Thatha. "You make some very good points."

"So, will you ban them?"

"It's not that simple," said Thatha. "I can't create a new rule just one week before the competition. That isn't fair."

"It's not fair on the planet either," said Sona. "You have to stop it!"

"My dear Jhansi Rani ..." started Thatha.

Sona knew that was a compliment. Jhansi Rani had been a brave queen who fought against injustice.

"... read the rule book," he continued. "If there's an existing rule I can use to ban chemical colours, plastic and glitter, I'd gladly do it."

Sona jumped up and struck a pose like the real Jhansi Rani. "Here comes Sona Rani to look after the planet!" she cried as she pretended to ride away on a horse.

Sona grabbed the rule book from Thatha's desk and went to her room with Elephant.

"This is not really a book, is it?" asked Elephant. There were only four pages.

"It's a pamphlet," said Sona, "of rules."

"So, it's a rule pam-ph-let," said Elephant. "That's hard to say."

1. *Each team can have no more than two participants and a helper.*

2. *The maximum size of each kolam is 5ft x 5ft.*

3. *The kolam design must not be demeaning.*

4. *The kolam must be traditional in spirit, regardless of the design.*

Sona pulled out a red pencil from her desk and underlined the words she hadn't understood: participants, maximum, demeaning and traditional.

Still, nothing in the rules mentioned anything about the materials that could be used. So, if the President and others were to use chemicals, glitter or plastic decorations, they wouldn't be breaking any of the rules.

The next morning was like any other morning: Appa busy getting ready for work, Amma busy with music practice, Paatti busy in the kitchen and Thatha busy helping Paatti in the kitchen. Sona was busy getting ready for school. She packed the kolam competition pamphlet in her bag.

During the morning break, Sona showed it to her friends.

"What is this?" asked Renu.

"A rule pamphlet," said Sona.

"I like the sound of that," said Joy. "Rule pamphlet."

"Say that five times fast," said Renu.

"Rule pamphlet, rule pamplet, rule famphlet," said Joy.

They doubled up laughing.

"I guess we should call it the rule book," said Sona, "like Thatha does."

"Did you underline these?" asked Joy.

"I've got to look them up," said Sona. "Like we do after Reading Period."

"We'll help you," said Joy.

They wrote down the underlined words on a sheet of paper:

1. participants
2. maximum
3. demeaning
4. traditional

During lunch break, Renu, Joy and Sona pored over the dictionary in the library.

Joy looked up "participants".

participant *noun (pahr-tis-uh-puhnt)*
a person who is taking part in an activity or
event.

"I know! Your paatti and the President are
participants," said Joy. Miss Rao always said
that they should try to use a new word in a
sentence straight away.

Renu looked up "maximum".

maximum *adjective (mak-su-muhm)*
as great, high, or intense as possible or permitted

"The maximum homework I'd like to do is
zero," said Renu.

"I wish Miss Rao agreed," said Sona.

"What was your word, Sona?" asked Joy.

Sona was looking up "demeaning".

demeaning *adjective (dih-mee-ning)*
putting somebody in a position that does not
give them the respect that they should have.

"I don't get it," said Sona. "I'm not sure how to use it in a sentence."

The first period after lunch was English. Sona put up her hand. "Miss, I have a question," she said.

"I haven't even started the lesson yet!" said Miss Rao. "But what's your question?"

Sona leaned forward with the sheet of paper. "Joy and Renu and I were looking up some words in the dictionary," she said.

"That's good," said Miss Rao. "Learning new words improves your vocabulary."

"Uh-oh!" groaned Joy. "Now I've got to look up 'vocabulary'."

"Go on, Sona," said Miss Rao. "What were you going to ask?"

"I was looking up the word 'demeaning'," said Sona. "But I still don't understand what it means."

Miss Rao wrote the word on the flip chart.

"If something is demeaning, it insults someone or shows that person disrespect," she said. "Calling people names, or shaming them, is demeaning to them."

"Thanks, Miss Rao," said Sona.

Sona hadn't realized that looking after the planet would mean learning so many new words.

THE COMPETITION MUST GO ON

That evening, Sona picked up the rule book and sat with Elephant and Minmini.

Talking to Minmini helped Sona think.

"We must figure out a way to stop people using chemicals, plastic decorations and glitter in their kolams," said Sona. "The first rule doesn't help. The second rule doesn't help either."

"What about the third one?" asked Elephant.
"I'm not sure what 'demeaning' means. Can you use it in a sentence?"

"If you called me a chatterbox, that would be demeaning," said Sona.

"Even if it's true?" asked Elephant.

Minmini chuckled.

"Oi!" said Sona. "Let's think about the planet. How can a kolam be demeaning to the planet?"

"If chemicals are used to draw it?" asked Elephant.

"Maybe," said Sona. "I need to check."

"With whom?" asked Elephant.

"Th-th-th," Minmini gurgled.

"Brilliant idea! Thanks, Minmini," said Sona. "Let's talk to Thatha, the chief judge."

"Mmm," said Minmini.

Thatha was snoozing in his reclining chair, a newspaper rising and falling over his face like a mini-wave. Sona tiptoed over and touched the paper.

Thatha woke up with a start. "What brings you to my Kingdom of Naps?"

"The rule book," said Sona, holding it up.

"Is it a quiz?" asked Thatha. "I know all the rules. I can recite them from memory."

"OK, then, what's the third rule?"

"Is it the one about size?"

"No," she said and read loudly, "The kolam design must not be demeaning."

"There's no need to shout," said Thatha. "What about this rule?"

"I think this rule will help us ban chemicals, plastic decorations and glitter!"

"How?" asked Thatha.

"If a kolam is demeaning to the planet, it is not allowed in the competition," said Sona.

"Hmm," said Thatha. "But if someone draws a flower and fills it with colours made from chemicals, the flower is not demeaning to the planet."

"But the chemicals harm the planet," said Sona. "So they are demeaning." She was so angry she threw the rule book on the floor. "Thatha, are you on my side or not?"

Thatha picked up the rule book and handed it back to Sona. "I'm on your side," he said.

"Sorry," said Sona. "Why don't you just cancel the entire competition? Then both Mullai and I will be happy."

"But I wouldn't be," said Paatti, bringing a steel tumbler full of coffee for Thatha.

"The kolam competition keeps our traditions alive," said Paatti. "I can teach you how to make kolams and, when you are older, you can teach your children. It's our art and it's our culture. It's fun too."

"That's why I can't cancel the competition," said Thatha. "Your paatti loves to participate and she doesn't even mind about winning."

Sona lay face down on the sofa and closed her eyes.

Paatti stroked Sona's head gently. "A persistent ant can turn a rock into a pebble," she told her. "Keep at it. You'll find a way to save the planet and the competition."

Sona sat up and smiled. If Paatti believed in her, then she could do it.

"I'm going to check the rule book again," said Sona. "Maybe there's another rule that can help us." Sona wasn't going to give up on her mission to look after Planet Earth.

Sona went back to her room and told Elephant and Minmini everything.

"Show it to Minmini," said Elephant. "Maybe she can help."

Sona showed the rule book to Minmini.

Minmini stabbed the page with her finger.

"What is it?" asked Sona.

"She's pointing at the fourth word you underlined," said Elephant. "You didn't look up the fourth word."

Sona, Joy and Renu had only checked the first three. There was one more word left.

"Minmini, you're the best little sister ever!" said Sona.

"What is the fourth word?" asked Elephant.

"'Traditional'," said Sona, opening her dictionary.

> **traditional** *noun (truh-dish-uh-nl)*
> of or relating to tradition;
> handed down by tradition

"What does that mean?" asked Elephant.

Sona looked up 'tradition' to understand 'traditional'.

> **tradition** *noun (truh-dish-uh-n)*
> a long-established custom or belief that has been passed on from one generation to another.

"That's what Paatti said about learning to create kolams from her grandmother," said Sona. "She wanted to do the same and teach me and pass it on from one generation to another."

But Sona still didn't know how this would help her look after the planet.

"Why don't you ask a grown up who's not part of the competition?" asked Elephant.

Thatha was a judge. Paatti and the President were participants. That left Amma and Appa.

Thatha, Paatti, Amma and Minmini had gone to listen to a concert and Appa was in charge of Sona, Elephant and their dinner.

Appa went back and forth from the kitchen to the dining room, cooking and working on his laptop at the same time. He set the table and called Sona to dinner.

"Welcome to Restaurant Appa," he said. "Today's special includes veggie lasagne with a side of steamed potatoes. This is one of Amma's favourites."

Sona pierced a piece of lasagne with her fork. But her mind was on the word "tradition".

"Appa, what do you know about traditions?" she asked.

"They're something people follow and carry on following for a long time," said Appa. "Like we always eat with our right hand."

"So, traditions never change?"

"Of course, they can," said Appa. "If you know

they are better when they change. But there are good traditions, that we don't need to change."

"How about we break tradition and eat with our left hands today?" asked Sona.

"Left-hand eating is definitely not for me," said Appa.

"This is why Elephants have just one trunk," whispered Elephant. "No need to choose between right or left."

Sona giggled.

"Anyway, why are you asking about traditions?" asked Appa, spooning some potatoes onto Sona's plate.

"The kolam competition rule book says, 'The kolam must be traditional in spirit, regardless of the design'," said Sona. "What does that mean?"

"It means the kolams must be made the same way it was done a long time ago," said Appa. "Like Paatti does – with rice flour."

"Yes!" Sona raised her arm to cheer, forgetting that her fork was full of lasagne. The blob of food that went flying narrowly missed Appa and his laptop and landed on the wall.

"Phew! That was close," said Appa, shutting his laptop quickly.

"Sorry!" said Sona. "I'll clean it up."

That night when Sona went to say goodnight to Minmini, which she did every night, she whispered, "I know what to do now."

"About the lasagne stain on the wall that wouldn't go?" asked Elephant.

"No, not that," said Sona. "About the competition. But it's a secret. I'll tell you later."

"Mmm," said Minmini.

"Mmm," said Elephant. He liked secrets. Even if he didn't know what they were.

WHO WILL TELL
THE PRESIDENT?

As soon as Sona woke up the next morning,
she grabbed Elephant and the rule book
and ran downstairs to the garden.

Thatha was already picking flowers to use
in his prayers. Minmini was lying on a rug
on the grass.

"I found a way to stop chemicals, plastic
decorations and glitter being used in the
kolam competition," said Sona. "And
Minmini helped."

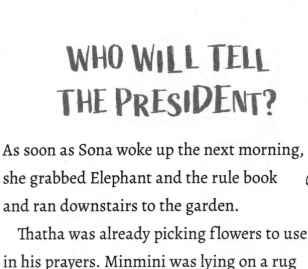

"I helped too," whispered Elephant.

Sona held out the rule book and said, "Please look at Rule Number 4."

Thatha read it, his brow furrowed. "What about it?"

Sona smiled. "Guess the meaning of 'traditional'," she said, triumphantly.

"I know the meaning, my hibiscus," said Thatha.

"Well, do you know what it means when it says, 'in spirit'?"

Thatha closed his eyes and hummed one of Saint Aandal's songs.

"When will he open his eyes?" asked Elephant.

"Any minute now," said Sona.

"Mmm," said Minmini.

"Do you mean that the way the kolam is drawn today should be similar to our ancestors' intentions?" asked Thatha, without opening his eyes.

"Yes!" said Sona. She knew Thatha would understand.

Thatha's brows were knitted tighter. "But we can't surprise the participants on the day of the competition," he said, opening his eyes. "We have to let them know ahead of time."

Sona's smile disappeared. "Why?" she asked. "It was in the rule book all along."

"But..." Thatha hesitated.

But before Thatha could finish his sentence, Amma called Sona to get ready for school.

"You have to find a way to look after Planet Earth, Thatha," said Sona, running back inside, "before I come back from school."

At school, Sona couldn't concentrate, not on Maths, Science or even her favourite subject, Art. She was thinking about what Thatha would do about Rule Number 4.

When Sona returned home from school, Thatha was dressed to go out. He was holding a clipboard and a pen.

"What did you decide?" asked Sona.

"Good news," said Thatha.

Just then, Paatti brought a glass of milk for Sona. "What are you two plotting now?"

"This is about the kolam competition," said Thatha. He held out the clipboard to Paatti. "Please read this and sign to confirm that you have understood the rules."

Sona looked first at Thatha, then at Paatti. What was on the clipboard?

Paatti read aloud. "Thank you for entering this year's kolam competition. We'd like to remind you of the following rules..."

Paatti looked up. "I already know all of this."

Thatha said, "Read on!"

"I draw your attention to Rule Number 4: 'The kolam must be traditional in spirit, regardless of the design.' Therefore, for the benefit of the planet, all kolams must be drawn using traditional materials like rice flour. Any entrant who uses chemicals, plastic decorations or glitter in a kolam will be disqualified. Please sign below to accept the terms and conditions."

Paatti smiled at Thatha and hugged Sona. "Well done, Sona," she said. "You've done it. You've brought back the joy of kolam."

"Will you sign?" asked Thatha.

Paatti laughed. "Of course," she said. "I've been following that rule for ever."

"One down, thirty-five more to go," said Thatha.

"I thought it was the entire neighbourhood," said Sona. "Why only thirty-five houses?"

"Because we have only thirty-five participants," said Thatha.

"Thirty-five is a good start," said Elephant.

Minmini and Sona grunted. But Elephant was right. Start small, start now!

Sona drank her milk as fast as she could, and picked up Elephant. Thatha was ready and waiting with his clipboard and a list of names.

As they stepped through the gate, Mullai arrived. "Is your amma in?" she asked.

"Nope," said Sona. "But I've good news for you. Remember you asked us to help you with the chemical kolam problem?"

"I remember," said Mullai. "You girls told me to get a flying auto-rickshaw."

"That was just a joke," said Sona. "But I think

I've fixed the problem. We're banning chemical colours, plastic decorations and glitter from the competition."

"That's great news, Sona," said Mullai.

"We're going to all the thirty-five houses who are in the competition to tell them that now," said Sona.

"Can I give you both a lift?" asked Mullai.

Sona shook her head. "No, that would be harmful to the planet," she said. "All the houses are on Thatha's morning choir route, so we're going to walk."

"That's right," said Thatha. "Walking is good for my health and for the health of the planet. Two mangoes with one stone."

"I'll walk with you then," said Mullai.

Soon Sona, Elephant, Mullai and Thatha had visited thirty-four houses on their list. Most people had agreed to the ban of chemicals, plastic and glitter. A few of them had dropped out saying they wouldn't be able to make enough rice flour before the competition. But they too agreed it was the right thing to do.

At last, they stood before the final house: The Orange.

Thatha rang the doorbell. Amma came to the door holding Minmini.

"Hello, family," said Amma. "Are you missing me already?"

"We came to see the President," said Sona. "But we do miss you."

The President looked up from her magazine when everyone trooped in.

"I have a notice for you to read, Mrs President," said Thatha.

"A notice?" asked the President. "Is it about the kolam competition?"

"Yes," said Thatha.

The President read the notice quietly, but her eyes shone like two angry comets. "What is this nonsense, and at the last minute too?" she asked. "Look at all the stuff I've bought already! I've spent a fortune buying all these."

Stacked in one corner of the room were bags of coloured powders, glitter and plastic decorations.

"Well..." Thatha began.

Minmini touched Sona's face.

Sona stepped up to the President. "I can explain," she said. "Didn't you say that we must all follow the rules established by our elders? That we can't change them every which way we want?"

The President stood up and started pacing like an angry lioness. "Yes, I did," she said. "That was—"

"Just for me?" asked Sona.

The President frowned. "Maybe you want me to drop out so your Paatti can win?" she said.

"Of course not," said Sona. "Paatti doesn't care about winning. She just wants all of us to keep on drawing kolams for ever and ever."

"Hmm," said Minmini.

"OK, I'm out, Mr Sharma," said the President. "I won't compete if you make a nonsense of the rules."

"But it's not nonsense," said Sona.

The President glared at Sona.

Sona wanted to make the President understand that she didn't need all the artificial and harmful materials to win the kolam competition.

Sona reached for the rule book and read the rules again.

"Do you have an assistant?" she asked the President.

"No!" replied the President. "Never!"

"Are you part of a team?" asked Sona.

"I'm a one-woman team," said the President, proudly.

Sona had an idea. "It says here that two adults plus an assistant can be in a team. You and Paatti can form a team and I can be your assistant," she said.

Amma and Mullai smiled at Thatha. Minmini giggled. But the President didn't say anything.

Thatha gave Sona a thumbs up.

With one hand, Sona held Minmini, and with the other she took the President's hand. The President still didn't say anything.

Sona's heart beat faster. But she knew that looking after Planet Earth meant doing difficult things – like convincing the President to follow the rules.

"Paatti and I were going to form the Golden Team. Now we can be the Presidential Golden Team."

The President grunted and then she turned to Sona and said in a low voice, "Kanaka won't want me."

"Paatti would love to be on your team," said Sona.

"Do you think so?" asked the President. "If she'll have me, I'd love to be on her team. In fact, I started using chemicals and plastic because she was so hard to beat."

"Now you can work together," said Thatha, holding out the clipboard.

The President signed the sheet and smiled. "I'd like that very much. I've always wanted to be on a team with Kanaka but I was too proud to ask."

"That's settled then," said Thatha. "Now we have a united family team!"

"Enjoy it while it lasts," said Amma. "Next year Mullai and I will enter the competition and we will win."

"And you'll have to enjoy it while it lasts too," said Sona, laughing. "When Minmini and I become a team, no one will ever beat us!"

When The President came home with Sona and told Paatti about the new Presidential Golden Team, Paatti made special burfis to celebrate. After dinner, the team held a meeting.

"I have an idea," said Sona. "How about we use the recycling symbol in our kolam?"

"What a brilliant idea!" said Paatti.

"And have you heard the story about how the squirrel got his stripes?" asked Sona.

"I know just the thing to draw," said the President, opening her notepad.

Sona had never seen the President so happy.

That night, when Amma had tucked Sona into bed, she said, "Paatti and the President in one team. That's a miracle."

After Amma left, Elephant said, "You made a miracle happen."

"We made a miracle happen," said Sona, "You, me and Minmini."

WINNERS AND PROTECTORS

Sona woke up early on the morning of the competition and ran downstairs with Elephant. The President and Paatti were discussing some last-minute preparations. Thatha had already left for the judges' meeting. Appa was the photographer for the day and had already left too.

"Good morning, Assistant," said the President.

"Good morning, Elephant," said Paatti.

"Good morning, Presidential Golden Team," said Sona.

Sona's job was to keep the cups of flour filled at all times and not get distracted.

"Ready?" asked Paatti. "Let's go."

They didn't have far to go. Sona opened the big gate and peeped out.

Each team stood in front of their house.

"Now we wash the street right in front of our house," said the President.

Sona poured water and Paatti swept the water and dust off the drawing space with a coconut-stem broomstick.

A volunteer cycled past with a whistle round his neck. Another volunteer walked past, checking that everyone was ready.

Amma and Mullai watched from the pavement on the opposite side of the street. Amma was holding Minmini and Mullai was holding Elephant.

Suddenly Sona felt nervous. Could she fill the cups fast enough? What if she couldn't and the President got upset with her in front of everyone?

The volunteer blew the whistle loudly. It was time to begin.

Paatti and the President laid their dots slowly and carefully. They had practised the same kolam over and over the night before. Sona kept filling their empty cups with flour.

Paatti and the President worked like the hands of a clock, moving without bumping into each other.

Just as Paatti stood up and stretched her back, the whistle blew.

Sona looked at their kolam and smiled.

A squirrel was holding a pebble, the symbol of Earth. The three lines on the squirrel's back, shaped like arrows of the recycling symbol, went all the way up the tail.

Sona was happy that Paatti and the President had chosen a design with a message about protecting Planet Earth.

"Thank you, Paatti. Thank you, President," said Sona.

"Thank you," said Paatti. "For reminding us to be good to our planet."

"And reminding us to work together," said the President.

"Will you enter as a team next year too?" asked Sona.

"Of course," said Paatti.

"Your amma and I will be entering too!" shouted Mullai.

"And we're going to win," called Amma.

"Don't crow before the sun rises," said Paatti, reminding Amma not to gloat before she'd actually won.

Soon the judges arrived with their clipboards. Thatha nodded at everyone as he jotted down notes.

"Hello, Thatha," said Sona.

"Shh!" said Paatti. "Now he is a judge, not your thatha."

When the judges had done their rounds, looking at and comparing all the kolams, the street volunteers blew the whistle again. The judging was over.

"Let's head to the local playground for the prize giving ceremony," said Amma.

The local playground was in the middle of the street, between their house and The Orange. As they entered through the gates, Joy and Renu ran up to Sona.

"We're excited to see if your paatti wins," said Joy.

"Paatti and the President and me," said Sona. "We're the Presidential Golden Team."

Everyone took their places facing the big wall behind the seesaw. A table had been set up with a projector. There was a microphone stand next to it.

Sona, Elephant and her friends stood at the front. Right behind them were Mullai, Amma and Minmini. Thatha and the other judges were discussing the results by the swings.

"When will they start?" whispered Elephant.

"Any minute now," said Sona.

Soon Thatha came to the table with the other judges to announce the winners.

The crowd hushed.

"Good morning, everyone! Welcome to this year's kolam competition prize-giving ceremony," Thatha began. "This year has been a little different for the participants. You might have noticed that none of the kolams contained any chemical colours, plastic decorations, ornaments or glitter."

Sona turned to look at the crowd. Many were nodding and smiling.

"We will continue to enforce this rule," said Thatha.

Mullai cheered.

"When will he tell us if you won?" whispered Elephant impatiently.

"Any minute now," said Sona.

Thatha cleared his throat. "Third prize goes to Mrs Anne Johnson and Sheeba," said Thatha. "Their kolam showed Planet Earth held up by many hands."

Everyone clapped as Mrs Anne Johnson and Sheeba came to the front.

"Bear with me. I'm going to announce the first prize now," he said.

Sona didn't know why Thatha was announcing the winners out of order. But Thatha always knew best.

"Mr Abdul Karim, the best tailor in this corner of the world and the best artist, wins the first prize this year," announced Thatha. "His kolam was a spinning wheel that had inspired our independence movement and our ancient tradition. The wheels depicted recycling symbols relevant for today."

Mullai whistled loudly and everyone clapped. Minmini clapped too.

Mr Abdul Karim ran to the front and took his position next to Mrs Anne Johnson. "Lucky the President dropped out," said Mr Karim. "She always wins."

The President waved to Mr Karim. "I didn't drop out," she called. "I'm part of a team this year."

"The second prize goes to a new team," said Thatha. "They were formed only a day ago and still managed to turn out a great kolam. The Presidential Golden Team – Kanaka, the President and Sona."

The team hugged one another.

"We won!" shouted Sona.

"Look!" said Sona, pointing to the screen.
Appa had connected his camera to the projector
so everyone could see the kolams.

Sona, Joy and Renu saw each kolam and
gasped.

"What is it?" asked Elephant. He didn't know
what they were all surprised by.

Sona pointed out the kolams to Minmini and Elephant. "See? Most of the kolams are about protecting the planet, just like ours," she said.

"We only asked people not to use chemicals, plastic decorations or glitter," said Sona.

"Maybe that inspired them to draw designs based on Planet Earth," said Joy. "And the rest of the neighbourhood has assembled to see these new kolams."

"Assembled..." mumbled Sona. "I've an idea!" she shouted.

Sona took Minmini from Amma's arms, then she pulled Renu and Joy and went up to the mic.

"Hello, everyone," Sona said, just like Miss Rao did in assembly. "We must look after Planet Earth and we need your help."

Sona explained how she had made a list of the things she wanted to change at home. "Maybe every family could try our new ideas?"

Many in the crowd nodded.

"We will put up posters," said Joy.

"And hand out leaflets," said Renu.

"And share our plan with all of you," said Sona.

"Yes!" shouted Mullai.

"Start small, start now!" shouted the President.

"Do more, do it now!" said Sona.

"Dddd," gurgled Minmini.

That night, Sona told Minmini about their plans to look after the planet. Joy is designing posters," she said. "And Renu is making a banner."

"Hmmm," said Minmini.

"You and I are going to make a plan with actions for everyone in our neighbourhood to follow."

"Can I help too?" asked Elephant.

"Of course," said Sona. "Are you both ready? I'm going to read all the ideas I've got."

"Number 1: Recycle plastics and don't buy any more disposable plastic items.

Number 2: Switch off lights and fans when not in use.

Number 3: Save rain water to water plants..."

And there were more...

"If we do all these things," finished Sona, "we can all look after our planet."

Minmini reached for Sona's hand and smiled.

Elephant whispered, "Sona Sharma – looking after Planet Earth."

NEW WORDS TO EXPLORE IN THIS STORY

burfi – rectangular or diamond-shaped sweet made with sugar and flour or sugar and coconut.

jalebi – a squiggly orange-coloured sweet made of sugar syrup.

kolam – a form of drawing in many parts of India and South Asia made with rice flour, chalk powder or rock powder, as well as other materials, like lentils and even flowers.

mridangam – a double-sided drum played by South Indian musicians that is made of a hollowed-out piece of wood from a jackfruit tree, covered on both sides with goat-skin leather.

pasuram – a verse, usually sung in praise of God.

sambhar – a lentil and tamarind dish that is perfect to eat with steamed rice.

LEARN TO DRAW
A KOLAM

1.

2.

3.

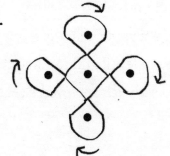

When Sona Sharma learns she is to become a big sister, she is determined to think up the perfect name for her new sibling. Sona may not be sure about sharing her beloved family, but she definitely wants to be the very best sister she can be.

"Told with warmth, humour and detail to ritual that will bring smiles of recognition across generations."
Sita Brahmachari

To make a peahen sing,
fight a champion wrestler,
solve the mystery of the holy man,
find the famous astronomer...

These are just some of the challenges
Prince Veera and his best friend,
Suku, face when they visit Peetalpur
for the summer festival. These clever,
funny trickster tales are sure to delight.

Chitra Soundar is originally from the culturally colourful India, where traditions, festivals and mythology are a way of life. As a child, she feasted on generous portions of folktales and stories from Hindu mythology. As she grew older, she started making up her own stories. Chitra now lives in London, cramming her little flat with storybooks of all kinds.

Jen Khatun's work is inspired by the natural world, the books on her shelves and the hidden magical moments found in everyday life. She says, "Being of Bangladeshi heritage meant that Chitra's story reminded me of the close bonds, traditions and memories of my family life. As a grown up, I cherish every profound life-teaching my family gifted me; they have made me who I am today."